Dirty CHRISTMAS

MIRA LYN KELLY
USA TODAY BESTSELLING AUTHOR

DIRTY CHRISTMAS is a sexy, feel-good standalone novella, set in the Slayers Hockey world.

As car-jackings go, I know I lucked out. But still.
Christmas is rough.
Now I'm stuck in some tiny twinkle-light town with my plans to avoid the holiday hype blown to *holly* hell.
I'm starting to suspect there's no escaping this lump of coal when a feisty redhead lands in my lap.
Suddenly, I know exactly what I want for Christmas.
Now I just have to convince her I'm not the naughty player she thinks I am and to give me a chance to score a permanent spot on her nice list.

DIRTY CHRISTMAS

Editor: Jennifer Miller

miralynkelly.com

Created with Vellum

DIRTY CHRISTMAS

A SLAYERS HOCKEY NOVELLA

MIRA LYN KELLY

MIRA LYN KELLY BOOKS, LLC.

1

Winter Break - Christmas Eve
Noel

As car-jackings go, I know I lucked out. But still.

I shoot a killing glare at my teammate as he grips the wheel in *my car* and swears before cutting around a mattress delivery truck going eighty-five. Diesel doesn't even blink.

Dick.

The problem isn't the speeding. Even headed out of the western burbs at Mach 5, this is Chicagoland and he's mostly keeping up with the midmorning traffic. Something I still can't seem to manage.

The problem isn't even that he shook me down for my keys in the O'Hare parking lot and forced his way into the driver's seat of my new Yukon, or that he's broken so many traffic laws, I've lost count.

The problem is that this fucker promised to spend our three-day break over Christmas with me and then had the nerve to tell me to get on the plane *alone* with some half-assed assurance he'd meet me in Vegas… when he finished stealing my car, I guess.

"Bullshit," I grumble, turning the heat for my side of the car up another degree and then turning his down by ten.

Diesel's knuckles go white, and for the first time since we peeled out of the parking garage, he spares me an apologetic glance.

"Sorry."

I cross my arms higher. Raise a brow. And wait like some pissed-off chick from one of the soap operas I don't really watch that often.

He blows out a tight breath. "You should've gotten on the plane, man."

Oh, that's what I should have done? "Yeah, that would have been awesome. Hop on the plane by myself. Kick it in Vegas. Over Christmas. Alone."

"Yeah, right, *alone*," he snorts. "You can't go to the grocery store without the checkout girl, bagger, and guy behind the deli counter sliding into your DMs before you leave. You would have had some babe sitting on your lap in the airport bar before the first drink even arrived."

"So?" You think I want to hang for the holiday with a bunch of strangers?"

He does a kind of double-take and then grits his teeth. After another high-speed half-mile and a blaring horn that has me twitching, eyes flashing to every possible point of collision around me, he shakes his head.

Jesus, what the hell is happening here? Twenty minutes ago, we were unloading our bags in the O'Hare airport parking garage, shooting the shit about what we were going to do in Sin City.

I was thinking we'd hit a Cirque show. I'm not really a gambler, but I'd be willing to blow some bank on roulette if that's what it took. Anything to pass the time until we'd clink our glasses for a single, "Merry Christmas," and then be done with the holiday until next year.

Diesel would have been perfect. Dude's not much for bunnies, or anyone else I've seen in the year since I got picked up as a defenseman for the Chicago Slayers, and he sounds about as enthusiastic about the holidays as I am.

Anyway, one minute I was locking the car, talking about getting a picture with the showgirls walking the strip, and the next, my generally chill teammate went bat shit.

Something crazy flickered in his eyes, and he demanded my keys, looking like he was about to take my head off when I gave him the keep-away treatment for less than two seconds. And then he was tossing his bag in the back, shoving me out of the way to climb in the front, and telling me to get on the plane without him.

Hard pass.

I've spent enough Christmases on my own, thank you.

The fucker nearly ran over my foot. Wouldn't wait for me to come round front, forcing me to dive into the second row as he peeled out.

FYI, getting this six-foot-one frame into the front seat while he took the down parking ramp way too fast... not awesome. But I'm badass. Flexible as fuck. And Diesel deserved the slow-motion roundhouse he took to the head while I got situated anyway.

Twenty minutes later, I still don't have an explanation for Diesel's GTA cosplay beyond the grunts and half-started sentences that never complete, so I ask again, "What the hell's going on? And who's in the blue Taurus we're following?"

No answer.

Then, without warning, we cut across two lanes of speeding traffic and take the exit fast enough that I'm pretty sure the Oh Shit handle's about to come off in my grip.

By the time I choke my heart back down into my chest and pry my eyes open, we're in some small town near the highway, parked with one tire on the curb of what I'm guessing is Main Street. And

Diesel's sprinting through a doorway tucked between a couple shops with twinkle lights framing the windows.

Shit.

I climb out and follow, ending up in a small entry/mailroom.

Empty. And the security door to the apartments upstairs locked.

I dick around for a second, contemplating pushing all three call buttons when the door to the street opens behind me, and a redhead with her hair up in one of those sexy-as-fuck messy knots blows in with half a dozen shopping bags in hand. She stops short and, cheeks rosy from the cold, stares at me with the widest, greenest eyes I've ever seen.

Damn. She's gorgeous, and with a chunky scarf in the same evergreen as her eyes, red coat, and ginger hair, this girl looks like Christmas incarnate. I bet she bakes cookies and sings Christmas classics in the shower.

And the way she's loaded down with gifts, I'm guessing there's a big family holiday ahead. Boyfriend planning the big ask, maybe. Who the hell knows, but I like it for her.

"Oh, hey," she says, taking a hasty step back. "Can I help you?"

"I don't know. Think you can wrestle a pro-hockey player into my car and keep him there long enough to get him on a flight to Vegas?"

A smooth brow a shade darker than her hair wings up in a wry arch— *my kryptonite* —and I've changed my mind. No boyfriend. For the thoughts that raised brow stirs, I'm sincerely hoping this girl is single.

I grin. "Say yes, and there's a ticket for you in it too."

Her mouth drops open, but whatever shutdown she's about to deliver gets cut off by the muffled sound of arguing coming from upstairs.

We both move for the security door, which is stupid since only one of us has a key. I wave her ahead, and she inches past with her bags.

She gives me the side-eye.

"Who are you?"

"Noel. I'm with Diesel," I say, pointing up.

She stills, door halfway open, and turns to me with an unreadable look. "*Diesel?* Here?"

Barreling through the doorway, she takes the stairs two at a time, and yeah, with a response like that, I have to follow.

~

Misty

No freaking way is Diesel, *the* Diesel of my sister's Do-Not-Mention-Vegas misadventures actually here, in our apartment.

Did they somehow reconnect in Seattle while she was interviewing? But then why would he be here? Fighting with her. Ugh.

I reach the second floor with this Noel in tow. He's big, like really big, and I half expect him to steamroll right over me, but he hangs back. The door to our place is open, the voices inside quieter now but still coming with some urgency. Not the alarming kind where I need to barge in there. I've been accidentally overhearing my big sister's conversations since she was old enough to have anything good to listen to, and this is not an intervention-level engagement.

But I've waited a year to find out what happened on that trip, and no way am I walking in and risking Stormy's already tight lips clamping shut even tighter when she sees me. So, I inch closer to the door on tiptoes, straining to catch a bit of the tea she won't willingly share with me.

Rude. I know. But we're only a year apart, and this is how I roll. She wouldn't expect anything less.

"Get anything good?" I startle at the too-close, too-gruff whisper and turn to find Noel beside me, one heavy shoulder propped against the wall, bulging arms folded over his chest, and his powerful legs casually crossed.

I blink. This guy is seriously hot and built like whoa. Even beneath the bomber jacket and jeans, there's no missing that muscular frame.

He's got dark hair that's falling in loose, overlong curls around his face, a crooked nose, and a lopsided grin that's so contagious, I find myself smiling in return and revising my assessment. He's a seriously hot *goof*.

Unraveling those big arms, he signals for my bags and then sets them carefully at our feet.

Our eyes meet, and we lean in to listen.

"She's saying something about them having an agreement, and he said he just wants to talk," I whisper.

Noel nods, not looking away. His eyes are the color of dark roast coffee, and the way he's watching me has a warming effect to match.

I clear my throat. "Were you in Seattle with her?"

Noel shakes his head, and a tousled curl falls over his brow. "My buddy saw her in the parking garage at O'Hare. Lost his shit. Stole my car. Ditched our flight. Blew my plan to escape. And followed her to wherever we are."

"Wow. Lots to unpack there."

"Right?" Then, "Who is she?"

"Stormy? My sister and roommate." At least until she moves. "And we're in Chestnut Hill. Who's Diesel?"

A little dent forms between his brows, like maybe he's not so sure he wants to tell me.

The look I give him has him quickly reconsidering.

Thought so.

"Whoa, easy there," he says, hands coming up with his smile. "He's my buddy and teammate. And I have no idea how he knows your sister."

"Vegas."

He looks past me to the open door. "She's coming to Vegas with us?"

"No, she met him there last year. But aside from his name, that's all I know." Though the way she'd said it and the weird mood she'd been in for the month after the trip had been enough to figure out that whatever went down had been good.

"We don't know much."

I shrug. "It's driving me nuts."

He cocks his head and gives me a grin. "So enough about them. Who are you?"

I laugh. "Um, not interested."

This guy has player written all over him. Not my thing, hot or not.

"Cool, me neither. I'm heading to Vegas when my boy wraps it up with your girl. But I figure, while we're waiting, why not make a new friend." He leans forward. "What's your favorite snack?"

"What are you, five?" I laugh, turning to face him.

"Twenty-five. And a half. You?"

This is ridiculous. But I can't even hear Diesel and Stormy anymore, and well, even if I'm not interested, which I'm definitely not, there's something about this guy that puts me at ease. He's got a friendly vibe to him, so I throw him a bone. "Twenty-four. And a quarter."

His grin spreads, showing off a criminally cute dimple, and I figure what the hell. "And my favorite snack is white cheddar popcorn. Why do you ask?"

"There's this challenge going around social, where you go to the store with a date and buy each other stuff from this list. I haven't done it, but I like the questions. Favorite drink?"

"Hot cocoa."

His head tips back as he lets out an appreciative moan, giving me a peek at the thick column of his neck. Nice.

When his eyes meet mine again, there's an intensity to them… I think.

"This is important. Whipped cream or marshmallows?"

Okay, maybe not so intense. But even so, I try to firm up my stare to mirror his. "Marshmallows. Mini."

He nods. "Marry me."

"Wow, not too choosy, are you?" I laugh, feeling the tension of the last few weeks ease the littlest bit. And sort of wishing this guy wasn't heading off to Vegas quite so fast. Because it's nice to laugh, and with all the weighty decisions about whether I should move too, it's been a while.

Suddenly, Stormy and Diesel are in the doorway,

both still wearing their jackets and looking as shocked to see us as I am to realize I'd completely forgotten about listening to them.

I straighten and force a wide, hopefully innocent smile. "Hey, guys, we were just—"

"Trying to listen in," Noel says unapologetically. "We didn't hear anything good, though. Too busy falling in love ourselves." He steps up to my side and slings an arm around me with a wink. "Dude, I'm taking Stormy's sister here—"

"Misty," I offer, half bracing for the usual crack about my parents watching the weather channel too much, but it doesn't come.

"—Misty, to Vegas with me. We're getting married, celebrating with a hot chocolate-mini marshmallow fountain, and doing all the shit you said no to. You're off the island."

The silence holds for a beat, and then, without responding, Diesel turns to Stormy. "All I'm asking for is an hour."

Blowing out a tight breath, she nods. "Fine. But not here."

I did not hear that right. "You're leaving?"

Giving my hand a squeeze, she meets my eyes. "I'll explain when we go over to Mom and Dad's this afternoon."

Diesel looks at Noel. "Can you push the flight?"

"Yeah, man. Whatever you need."

We watch them leave in awkward silence. And then Noel turns to me.

"Sure you don't want to take me up on the Vegas wedding? You'll have to drive to the airport. Pretty sure Diesel just stole my car again."

2

Noel

Nailing the perfect fold, Misty takes the inch tab of tape stuck to the tip of my finger and shakes her pretty head. "No. I'm still not marrying you."

She secures the wrapping paper and then starts in on the bow. I press on the half-tied knot, and she finishes. Nearly an hour in and we've got a system.

"But if you don't have a good reason to eliminate me as a contender— like you aren't into NHL players, or you have some hard-and-fast rule against charming, confident guys who make you smile—"

Elbows resting on the small round table in the corner of her kitchen, she laughs. "*Listen* to you."

Damn, I dig that sound. I dig this girl with her funky mugs— she gave me her favorite. A picture of

Bob Ross with a black background that turned into a landscape when she poured the hot chocolate in—and generous, welcoming personality.

She could have left me on the couch or out in the hall, but instead, she sat me down and started to chat while we wrapped her presents. She works in billing for a dentist down the street but wants to find a new job because she hates the sound of the drill. I told her I play hockey for the Slayers, and she thought it was cool but doesn't know much about sports. I said I'd marry her anyway, but she's still not sold.

"Then why say no? Sure, if you've found a deal-breaker, share it with the class." I wait, watching her for tells, like the slight blush pushing into her cheeks and the way she slides that mostly empty mug of cocoa around, this way and that. "Have you?"

Those striking green eyes meet mine from beneath the fringe of her thick lashes. "No."

It's low-key flirty, and I give myself a mental high-five.

"See, we're practically engaged," I tease, pulling my phone out to check my messages. Because as much as I'm digging this girl, eventually she's going to take off for the family holiday, and I'd really like to be taking off for Vegas before then.

"Still nothing?" she asks.

"Nope. Probably on his way." He better be. Our

flight's at two. "And if we don't catch this one, there'll be a few flights out later tonight."

She takes a big breath. "Yeah, but it's Christmas Eve. You don't want to spend it on a plane."

Pushing out of my chair, I take my mug and hers — which is shaped like a bomb with a capital letter F printed on it. I think I love this girl —over to the sink and wash them out. There's a small window above it, looking down to Main Street where the flurries that started falling a while ago have left a fine dusting of white over the sidewalks, cars, and road below. "The plane's fine. Just so long as I'm not sitting in the hotel bar alone."

That's rough and an experience I'd rather not repeat.

She comes to stand beside me, her back to the counter, slender hands tucked into the front pockets of her jeans. "No family for either of you?"

"Diesel's not close to his and mine is all gone, so when he mentioned Vegas, I was like, 'Hell, yes. Count me in.'"

"Gone?"

I can hear the concern in her voice, and man, it's not what I want, so I keep it as concise as possible. "Lost my parents a few years ago in a boating accident."

"Noel, I'm so sorry."

"It's been a long time, but thank you."

"No other family?" When I shake my head, she sighs. "The holidays must be really tough."

I don't usually talk about this stuff, but for some reason, standing here beside Misty, I don't mind.

"Hey, you're a sweetheart, but don't worry about me. Most of the year I'm good. And all the Christmas season festivities leading up to the big day are hella fun. I love Christmas parties, rock the ugly sweater, and have a blast buying gifts for my friends. Oh, and the cookies." I hum and nod. "Give. Me. The. Cookies."

She gives up another one of those musical laughs. "Yeah?"

"Yeah. It's all good. It's just that part where everyone starts to peel off, heading home to their families, that gets a little rough." It gets lonely. It gets sad. "Fast forward through all that, and the holidays are awesome."

"That what you're doing with Diesel?"

"Hoping to."

"I can see it." She squints at me. "Two pro-hockey hunks on the loose in Sin City. I'm betting there isn't any shortage of girls looking to keep you company until tomorrow comes."

I feign shock. "When I'm freshly engaged to you? Not a chance."

"Sure thing, *ladies' man*."

I could correct her, but why when I'm leaving any minute? Or I hope I am. Where the hell is he?

Misty leans in to bump me with her shoulder. "What's it like there at Christmas?"

I set the mugs on the drying rack. "I'm betting it's a lot like Vegas any other day of the year. But maybe with a fuck-ton of over-the-top decorations." And then, because I'm pretty sure she'd be disappointed if I didn't, I add, "Come with and see for yourself."

There's that smile again.

"I would, seeing as how we're *engaged* and all, but—"

"Family. Holidays. Totally get it. It's not me. It's all that."

Her eyes are pretty when she rolls them, but they're even prettier when they meet mine and hold, stirring something inside me I don't—

It doesn't matter.

I'm not staying. I barely know this girl. But, damn, there's something about her that won't let me look away.

At least not until her phone rings, and even then, she's the one to do it. But only after a beat of hesitation that shouldn't be nearly as satisfying as it is.

"Hey, where are you guys?"

Finally. "See, told you they were on their way," I whisper, but instead of another pretty eye roll, I get a look packed with the kind of concern that sets my teeth on edge.

"Stormy, you can't just—"

It's just a delay. That's why she's calling.

I'll have to bump the flight a couple hours, that's all.

Except I know that's not all by the way Misty turns, shutting me out with her shoulder as she heads back into the living room.

"I know you do." She's dropped her voice to an urgent whisper, but I can still hear every word. "But what about—"

Fuck me.

She wants to know what to do about the jackass abandoned in her apartment. I can feel the heat crawling up my neck, practically see the pity that's going to be in her pretty green eyes—

"Bullshit!" she snaps at the phone that's already gone dark, and when she turns, it's not pity in her eyes at all.

Whoa. Misty's pissed.

Misty

OH, my blood is boiling now. I whirl around to face Noel, who's watching me with an expression I can't quite read.

I huff. "What's wrong with your buddy to leave you like that? And seriously, Stormy— it's Christmas Eve and, and—" I throw my hands up, no idea what to say. "She's not like this. She doesn't just not show up when she's supposed to."

"Hey, I'm sorry. Honestly, I have no idea what's going on with them, but this screws your plans too."

Noel's phone pings with a text, and when he checks it, his face stays blank as a slate.

"Douchey Diesel?"

His lips start twitching like he's trying not to laugh and, wow, he has a really nice mouth. Noel seems like a nice guy. Nicer than that douche Diesel for sure now, even though Stormy apparently thinks he's nice enough for whatever happened in Vegas to happen. And for whatever's going on today to go on.

Gah.

"Yeah, but he's actually a good guy."

"It's bullshit. But we're not going to let him ruin your night or mine." And before he can even ask, I hold up a hand. "But don't get any ideas. I'm still not going to Vegas with you."

This time his laugh is the real thing, and as much as I don't want to admit it, it does a little something to me. Not enough to act on. No way. But so what if he's one of those guys who never turns it off? He's funny and kind of sweet, and his flirting feels good.

But instead of asking what I have in mind, he shakes his head and thumbs through his phone.

Craning forward, I peek at what he's doing.

No way.

"Hey, forget Uber," I say, pushing his phone down. "It's Christmas Eve. Stormy said she'd be home tonight. Hang out with me until Diesel picks you up. We can do Christmas stuff!"

"Aww, Mistletoe, you're a sweetheart to worry about me. But I'm good."

He almost looks like it too. But even in the little time we've spent together, I know better. "What if I'm not?"

Now I've got his attention.

"Why aren't you good?"

"My plans for Christmas Eve just took off with your ride. I've been stood up."

His dark brows draw forward. "What about your family?"

"Flying in tomorrow morning. Stormy and I were going to decorate their house tonight so it was ready for tomorrow, but now I'm on my own."

"No boyfriend?"

"Really? We're engaged, and you ask me this now? No."

There was a guy, but to call him a boyfriend would have been a stretch. And after a few uninspiring dates, I knew there wasn't anything there. Truth is, I've got more of a connection with Noel after an hour than I had with Richie after a month.

Not that I think it's going anywhere.

It's clear that Noel is a relentless flirt, but it's just as clear he's not serious when he does it. The guy plays for the Slayers. Something tells me he could have a date before I could snap my fingers. Not just any date, either. Probably a model. Someone who only uses one name.

"How about you? Girlfriend?" If she's on a shoot or based out of Paris, it would explain why he isn't with her for Christmas Eve. I know better than to assume.

When he shakes his head, that smile going a little lopsided, I can't help it.

"What was your last girlfriend's name?"

"Patty." He leans in conspiratorially. "Why, planning to check my references?"

"Please." Patty is not a supermodel's name. I don't think. Whatever. "Just figured it was probably one of your challenge-turned-getting-to-know-you questions. And if we're going to be hanging out, we might as well be friends."

He gives me a slow nod, his smile spreading. "I like it."

"Good, then what do you say we get started?"

"What do you wanna do first?"

"I want to get a tree." I wave over to my Chia Tree with its little red light-up star next to the coffee maker. "This guy is cute, but I want the real deal."

There's a strange glint in Noel's eyes. "A live tree?"

"We always cut one down with my parents, but the tree farm is almost an hour from here. This year they were just talking about getting something small at a local stand. But if you're game, we could drive out and—"

And that's as far as I get before Noel is whipping his coat on and grabbing mine to help me into it. Rubbing his hands together, he presses a quick, grinning kiss to my cheek. What a flirt!

"Let's do this!"

3

Misty

He's a puppy.

A huge, six-foot-something, gotta-be-two-hundred-pounds-of-pure-muscle puppy, running back and forth between the shack where we picked up the saw, the tree shaker, and the baler in the front lot of Falter's Trees like he doesn't know what to play with first.

"They have hayrides!" he calls, pointing to where a couple families with small kids are climbing down near the shop.

I laugh, trying to imagine what this guy must have been like as a kid. Because as an adult, he's over-the-top excited. He's ridiculous. And cute and fun and—

God, I am not catching feelings for this *player*.

Sure, talking to him is astonishingly easy considering we just met this morning. And not just about the getting-to-know-you trivia and off-the-wall assertations of love and marriage, either, though that's definitely fun. Even when he's leaning over my seat, promising it to the woman at the drive-thru if she'll hold the mayo on his sandwich.

But the *real stuff*— the parts where we talked about what it's like being the new guy on the team, how Stormy's plans to move to Seattle are making me question my own plans, and how intimidating it can be as a player to know that the *if* and *when* of whether he moves is decided by someone other than him... Those quiet truths that don't come easy with anyone, let alone virtual strangers, seem to come as naturally as breathing between the two of us.

It doesn't feel like we're strangers now, though.

I watch as Noel runs back to the small welcome shed where a shriveled little woman who has to be in her seventies if she's a day is handing out maps of the farm. He asks her a question and she points to the map, which earns her a hug and a kiss on her cheek that has her giggling like a schoolgirl. And he tells her he'd marry her if he wasn't already engaged to me.

It's adorable. *It's fun.* And a good reminder. Guys like Noel aren't serious, and I'm a pretty serious girl. At least about relationship stuff. So, no crushy feelings.

Shaking my head, I revert to teasing. "Think you can *handle* a hayride?"

His mouth drops open in mock affront before curving again into that lopsided grin he wears so much.

"Asks the terror of highway hell," he says, now headed my way.

"I drove at a *snail's pace*!" Seeing the way his eyes are fixed on me, my heart does a little flip as I take a retreating step. "And still you were pumping your imaginary brake pedal and grabbing the dash."

He keeps closing in. "That car cut us off."

"You *clotheslined* me," I accuse a little breathlessly. "And that car was a half-mile ahead of us."

He stops in front of me, close enough that I need to look up to see his face. Close enough that a part of me is wondering if he'll come even closer. If maybe I'd like it if he did, even if I know I shouldn't.

It doesn't mean anything. And so long as I remember that, it's totally fine.

"I was saving you," he says, quieter now, eyes holding mine. And then he does it. Leans in just that much more, and it's like some kind of magnetic energy between us, because then, I'm leaning too. His eyes drift lower, to my mouth, lower still, to— *to the saw* he takes from my grasp.

His brows bounce. "Let's find a tree."

We walk through row after row of snow-dusted spruce, balsam, Frasers, and white pine, talking and laughing and rejecting each other's tree picks until finally we've found her.

"Look at you, beautiful." Noel walks a slow, assessing circle and bites his bottom lip, giving this tree bedroom eyes so sexy I'm embarrassed to admit I feel a flutter in my belly. "Tall, full backside. I just want to run my hands over—"

"Noel, do you need a minute alone? Or do you want to get your hands out of her branches and cut her down?"

"Jealous?"

"Insanely," I deadpan. And no, I'm not jealous of a tree, but I am reminding myself that eventually Diesel and Stormy are going to show up, and when they do, Noel's going to leave. He's going to hop on a plane to Vegas, where he'll be giving his best flirt to some other girl. Maybe one who isn't as serious as me. One who will get to find out what a night in this man's arms would feel like. And maybe... I'm a little jealous of her?

No. That's crazy.

Crazy like the way Noel's kneeling on the blanket I keep in my Jeep, caressing the trunk of the tree he's about to cut down and asking if that's the spot she likes, whether she wants it fast or slow while giving me a salacious wink.

This guy!

I want more of this man, yes. Because it feels like

we're becoming friends, and that is something I want to keep.

And the only chance I have of that happening is to tamp down any sort of crushy feelings that might be creeping in and trying to take root.

"Hey, Mistletoe, hold my stuff?" he asks, peeling off his jacket.

I nod, stepping around the cut trunks of trees and branches left behind to take it.

I open my mouth to say something but freeze when he starts undoing his fitted charcoal button-up next, shrugging out of one massive shoulder and then the other, leaving him in a tight white T-shirt that hugs every sculpted muscle beneath.

It's the sort of hard-core sexy, masculine move I thought only existed in those slow-motion black-and-white video clips of unknown origin that turn up in your feed from time to time. But it's real, and I really need to close my mouth and swallow before I start to drool.

No crushy feelings!

Clearing my throat, I try for a casual I'm not feeling. "Shouldn't you keep that on? It's freezing out here."

"Hockey player, remember?" He hands over the shirt, still warm from his body. "Besides, it can't be colder than thirty."

And snowing. "Thirty is T-shirt weather for you?"

He gives me a low laugh and a smile that's possibly more distracting than that snug-fitting T-shirt. "Not as a rule, but playing hockey on the lake behind my house as a kid, there was a time or two, at least. Besides, Diesel's got my luggage. So, nothing to change into if this stuff gets wet or dirty."

Do not think about what it would be like to get *wet* and *dirty* with this man.

He points to the tree. "You want a turn?"

"Not unless you need a break."

He laughs and starts to saw, biceps flexing hard enough I'm concerned for the wellbeing of the T-shirt stretched taut around them.

No. Crushy. Feelings.

The tree falls and, victorious, Noel springs to his feet, pumping his fist… and that poor T-shirt is soaked through from the snow and plastered to his sculpted chest and abdomen.

Damn.

Noel turns, and I am so busted.

But I don't want to make this weird. How do I *not* make this weird?

I gulp. His brow lifts.

It's *so* weird.

Damage control time. "*That's* what your stomach looks like?" I say with all the bravado I can muster. Going for bold and brash, I wave a hand toward him, twirling my finger in the air. "You've *gotta* let me see for real. Shirt up, pretty please!"

I want to die, but I keep that too-bright smile on my face.

He looks down at himself and then to me, eyes narrowing. Suspicious. And rightly so, but no way am I owning up to my crushy fluster. So, I double down. "Wait, can I touch it?"

Okay, he clearly has no idea what to make of this. Finally, he looks around and, seeing we're alone on this part of the farm, gives a shrug.

"Sure, why not?"

Um, because I'm a creeper? *Just say no, Noel!*

But he doesn't, and now I feel guilty. I'm pretty sure I want to do the right thing here, but maybe it would be worse to change my mind. And I don't want to bruise his ego.

Snow crunching beneath my boots, I walk the few feet to where he's bunched his shirt, and holy shiznit, what lies beneath is even more impressive.

My hand is reaching before I even realize it's taken on a mind of its own, and startled, I pull it back. "Ack, I feel like a perv."

Stupid conscience.

Noel just laughs and takes my hand, using it to pull me in a step. Definitely inside the bubble here, and I'm looking up at him again, getting caught in that same eye contact that's been snaring me on and off throughout the day.

Slowly, he brings my hand to his mouth and, oh my, he *breathes* warmth over my fingers.

I shudder, my brain scrambling as his smile hitches higher, and he breathes again. Then, "Just warming them up first."

I nod.

Watch the air fog the space where his hand holds mine. His thumb brushes the length of my finger, and my heart stops. And then he's pressing my palm to the hard ridges of his stomach, letting my fingers tuck into the valleys alongside.

"*Whoa.*"

He laughs again, and the landscape beneath my touch shifts and bunches. "I do a lot of core work to protect myself from injuries." His hand covers mine. "You good, or you need another minute?"

"I'm not sure an hour would be enough." Or a week. Or maybe even a year. "That's nuts."

"I've got a weird job. It's one of the benefits, I guess." Plucking my hand from his body, he gives it a quick squeeze and adds, "Pretty girls feeling me up, I mean."

Annnd my face is on fire. This is going to be so weird.

~

Noel

IT'S OFFICIAL. This isn't me chatting Misty up like I chat up everybody else. Nope. This is the real deal.

I'm into her. And it's not just because she put her little icicles all over my wicked-hot washboards, either.

That's not new. Since getting voted hardest abs in the league, I've got bunnies hustling for a feel after every game. The way I reacted to *her* hand pressed against me, though? That was definitely new. Different. I wasn't counting down the seconds until I could give her a polite smile and move on. No. The only reason I broke off that touchy-feely bit of fun was because Not-So-Little Noel was about to make a scene.

Don't get me wrong, I wouldn't be opposed to a private meet-and-greet at some point. But not until I get a sense of whether Misty's feeling me the way I'm feeling her. And if it does happen, it sure as hell isn't going to be in the middle of a Christmas tree farm in broad daylight.

Which is why I hoist our tree over my shoulder and head for the Jeep, keeping the showing off to the bare minimum of what my ego demands.

Back at the lot, we hand the tree off to a couple kids from the family-run business. I whip off my T-shirt and yank on my dress shirt and jacket while they bale the tree and then I help tie it to the roof, double-checking the knots.

"Noel, these guys are pros. Seriously, that tree isn't coming off."

These "pros" are probably fifteen.

I check it again, then head in with her to the warming shed to settle up.

Two steps inside, I stop in awe. It's a Christmas wonderland. Fresh garlands and wreaths scent the air, draped around a cozy space packed with handmade ornaments, candies, and preserves, and more holiday-themed kits and decorations than I've ever seen in one place. And to the right, there's a blinged-out tree with a few wrapped gifts beneath and an easy chair with a posted sign saying that Santa is on break.

"I could fill in." I lean closer, dropping my voice to a low rumble. "Let you sit on my lap and tell me all the things you want."

I'm getting dangerously addicted to those eye rolls. Especially when they come with that hot blush.

Leading me over to the hot cider and cookie bar, she fills a couple small paper cups with the scalding cider. "It's not just about the tree when we come here." She hands me a sugar cookie on a paper napkin and looks around with a reverence that tells me more than words about what this place means to her. "This is how you do it. You eat your cookie and walk around the shop until your cider is cool enough to drink. Stormy and I got to choose one new ornament a year and then spent the rest of our time picking which caramel to buy for the ride home."

I take a bite of my cookie and let the warmth of the cider seep into my hands, imagining Misty as a cute little kid with her family here. And then imagining something else.

"My parents would have loved this place." I never volunteer information about them. Don't like to invite conversation about them. But for some reason, standing here with this girl I barely know, I do. I can.

Misty blows on her cider, her eyes soft as they meet mine. "They were big on the holidays?"

I'm hit with the ache in my chest that usually has me running for a distraction, and... for the first time in years, I don't want to escape it. I want to dig into the memories of my mom with flour on her face, laughing while she iced cookies for my team. I want to hold on to the echoes of my dad tearing a recipe out of his French cooking magazine and reading the ingredients off like it was a novel that had him hooked.

I rub at my chest and breathe, let myself feel it all.

"Oh yeah. Holidays were huge in the Nichols' house. Christmas most of all. The lights would go up the day after Thanksgiving. We had Advent calendars and those little North Pole villages with the trains and moving parts. Christmas music piping through the house. It was great." And then they were gone and there was nothing. Not even the memories, because I'd do anything to avoid them. But not now.

"You okay?" she asks gently. "We can go."

I shake my head. "No way. It's nice to do this. I've missed it."

Her smile spreads, and she wraps her hand around my arm, pulling me along. "Good, because you haven't even seen the gingerbread house bar yet."

"That good?"

"You know the Lego store, with the zillion bins of every piece in every color you can imagine?"

"Come back to my place and I'll show you my Lego Death Star."

She gives a little bounce, ignoring my cheesy line. "Think that, but with candy! We're totally building one when we get to my parents' place."

"I like it." I like her. A lot.

I like the look of her, yeah. A lot. But I like what she *says* more.

I like that she makes me laugh and the things that make her smile. I like that she's smart and bold and a bit of a spitfire. I like that she sings along to the radio and that her laugh sounds like music. I like the way the air feels between us when our eyes meet... and I like that she's the type to hang out with me for the day because my dickhead-but-not-actually-a-bad-guy teammate dropped my ass on her doorstep and abandoned me.

And I really like when she looks at me like she did when we first got to the farm. Because that look wasn't about the cheap wet T-shirt stunt I pulled later when I cut the tree down— yeah, I'm not proud —or what I do for a living or what's in my wallet. That look was curious, and I think it might even have been a little interested too.

4

Misty

By the time we make it to the isolated road leading down to my parents' place at the lake, it's after four. The snow's been coming down in earnest for a while now, but the reason I'm subtly giving in to a sigh of relief is less about the driving conditions and more about the larger-than-life man who's occupying more than my passenger seat.

He's too much.

Too easy to talk to.

Too good at making me laugh.

Too close for me not to notice how incredible he smells or how surprisingly sexy the broken line of his nose is. Or how every now and then it feels like the too-small space between us has taken on this subtle charge that's scrambling my brain.

"Plows don't get out here?" Noel asks as we slowly navigate the treelined road.

"We're outside town, so not the regular ones. There's a guy who clears the roads in the area, but sometimes it takes a while for him to get to our little lane." I take the turn down our driveway and smile when the motion sensor trips the outside lights, illuminating my parents' house.

"Nice place. This is where you grew up?"

Pulling to a stop in front of the attached garage, I cut the engine. "Yep. Usually, we've got the whole frame of the house strung with Christmas lights, but with my parents visiting my aunt, it's a little different this year."

I unbuckle and climb out, slipping a little but catching myself as I flip through the keys on my ring for the door key.

Noel rounds the vehicle, coming to my side. His big hand is light and steadying at my elbow as we walk up the front steps and then warm and distracting at my back as I let us in.

The house is chilly at first, with the thermostat set to fifty while my parents are gone. There's a light on in the kitchen and one in the upstairs hall, set to timers, so it's not that dark or spooky, but it's way easier walking into the emptiness with Noel at my side.

"I can't believe it's Christmas Eve," I mutter. "There should be Christmas music and a fire and my parents dragging out their hidden gifts from every corner of the house."

Noel gives a quiet nod beside me, and I want to kick myself for being so insensitive. "Noel, I'm sorry. That was—"

"That was nothing to apologize for. I like hearing what your Christmases are like with your family. It's reminding me of mine. And as much as I thought I didn't want that, it's really nice." He grins. "Besides, we're about to Christmas the shit out of this place. It's going to be awesome by the time your sister shows up. And tomorrow, when your parents are *ooh*ing and *ahh*ing over the holiday perfection, you can tell them your fiancé helped you out and—"

"I'm meeting him in Vegas that afternoon?"

"Nah." He shoves his hands in his pockets. "Stay here with your family. Soak it up... We've got the rest of our lives to run off together."

"You're a good guy, Noel." And the more time I spend with him, the more I like him... and even though I know better, it's in that flirty-feelings kind of way too.

He grins again, leaning close enough to my ear that I can feel his breath against the shell. "Don't let it get around."

Pressing a hand to where the butterflies have taken over my belly, I nod and force my legs to move.

I flip on a few lights and turn up the heat, keenly aware of Noel beside me. Trying to keep my eyes from constantly drifting to him, to his hands, his shoulders, his mouth.

Oh my God, stop looking at his mouth!

We open the garage so we can bring the tree in. When we've got it in the stand in the open spot where my dad's car would usually be parked, Noel cuts the twine.

I let out a sputtering cough as the branches bounce out, spraying bits of snow over us both.

Noel chuckles, brushing his chest.

"You barely got hit at all," I laugh, reaching out to help.

Except helping means that I'm running my hands over his hard-packed muscles, which wouldn't be so much of a problem if I'd just done it and stopped. Smiled and made a crack about his insane body like I did at the farm. But instead, the second I realize what I'm doing, those harmless brisk brushes cease, my movements turning molasses slow as he catches my hand in his.

He gives my hand a light squeeze. "Think I'm good."

Right. Of course, he is.

And I'm making it weird again.

"*Sorry.* The hazards of fresh trees," I whisper lamely.

God, this guy probably only agreed to come along with me because I seemed like a reasonably cool girl. Not reading too much into what I'm guessing is simply his chronically flirty personality. Now he's stuck in my parents' house with me on Christmas Eve and suddenly I'm touching his chest like it's mine, and—

"Hey." He crooks his finger beneath my chin, tipping my head so our eyes meet, and the breath stalls in my lungs. Gently wiping at my cheek with his thumb, he says, "Worth it."

He steps back, shoving a hand through his dark mane. "Jeep still open?"

It takes me a second before my brain reboots and I nod, managing a strangled, "Yeah."

"Let's get everything inside and then we can start on the decorations."

Noel

I ALMOST KISSED HER.

And maybe I would have if we'd been standing in some bar with half a dozen of her friends nearby instead of alone in her parents' place, which is remote enough I couldn't even see the neighbors when we pulled up.

So, no. That isn't part of the plan.

But damn, when she was looking up at me like that, lips parted and eyes searching—

Shit.

I read situations for a living. The ice, the players, every move and twitch tell me what's going to happen an instant before it does. It's what makes me good at my job.

But this?

This isn't a game. It's not just a job.

And I really don't want to misread what's happening here, only to realize the soft, searching look that felt like it was pulling me in like a tractor beam was actually Misty searching for signs of a serial killer within.

So, I'm going to wait until Diesel shows up with Stormy.

I'm going to play it cool, and then before we leave, which I'm seriously less enthusiastic about than I was this morning, maybe see about scoring her socials—

I stop halfway to the house, four oversized handle bags dangling on each arm and a box of wrapped gifts in my grasp, and turn to where Misty's locking up her car... with a key.

Which is almost as weird as me not having her socials plugged into my phone already.

Diesel might have lost his ever-lovin' mind this morning, but the guy was right about my habit of buddying up with damn near everyone I meet. How the hell have I spent the entire day with this girl and not managed to hustle her phone, Facebook, IG, or Snap?

"What's up?" she asks, hiking the strap of her bag over her shoulder.

"What's your phone number?"

She walks past me with a sigh. "You think just because we're engaged, I'm going to give you my number?"

My bark of laughter is swallowed by the falling snow, and I follow her inside, where we both kick off our shoes and brush the snow from our hair and shoulders.

Misty looks through the pane of glass in the front door. "It's really coming down out there." She wrinkles her nose. "I wish you could have seen it with the lights outside."

Me too, but I just shrug. "Next year. When we're married."

Damn, that pretty eye roll. Then, "You ready to do this thing?"

Hell, yes, I am. "Lead the way, Mistletoe."

There are a fuck-ton of decorations in totes in the basement. They aren't that heavy, but I totally flex carrying them up. Not that Misty notices. She's suddenly a woman on a mission, moving furniture around and clearing surfaces. Pointing out what decorations go where and only stopping when she gets to a special one to tell me the story behind it.

I could listen to her laughing and detailing exploits of her Christmases past all night. Longer.

When we've done everything but the tree, the place is transformed.

Fresh garlands with white lights wrap the banister, and stocking holders shaped like shiny wrapped presents sit on the mantel. Nesting bowls filled with candies from Falter's Trees replace the magazines and mail on the coffee table, and an Elf on the Shelf is poised for some pole dancing on a lamp in the corner.

I stack the empty totes together, leaving the one with the ornaments, and return them to the basement. When I come back up, Misty's standing at the top of the stairs with a worried look on her face.

"Hey, what's wrong?" I ask, reaching for her on instinct.

"Stormy just texted and they aren't coming tonight."

My chin pulls back, and I check my own phone. One missed text. Two words: *Sorry, man.*

Shit.

I look up at Misty and push a smile I'm not feeling to my face. That's it. They're not coming. Which means I'm not waiting on Diesel and it's time for me to go.

I'm not ready. Not ready to give up this thing between us or the magic of a holiday I haven't let myself experience in years.

"You're leaving?" she asks quietly.

"I'll bring the tree in for you, but it looks like you're going to be on your own with the ornaments."

Arms crossed over her chest, she doesn't look any happier about it than I am. Only unlike this morning, when she'd been beautifully pissed on my behalf, now, she just looks a little sad.

"Well, but what are you going to do?"

"First thing? Get your digits, Mistletoe." I hand her the phone. "I want a picture of you and the fam in front of the tree tomorrow."

Her thumbs move over the screen, and her phone lights up with the text she sent herself. She doesn't look at me, and something in my chest tears open.

"And what are you going to send me a picture of?"

I think about Vegas. I could get an Uber to the airport. Catch the next flight and be there before midnight. I could, but I know I won't.

"My apartment. Maybe I'll get my Uber to stop at a tree stand. Pick up the last spindly Charlie Brown tree on Christmas Eve and bring it home."

She nods, still not giving me her eyes. And I want them.

"I'll make microwave popcorn and use one of those hotel sewing kits I've got in my bathroom drawer to string a garland."

A laugh, but not what I'm craving.

Then, quietly, "You don't need to go."

"Yeah, I do." I take a deep breath, letting it out slow. "But I want you to know, spending today with you has been incredible. It meant a lot to me. So, thank you." I press a kiss to her cheek before stepping back to order a car.

A minute later, my gut knots, and I mumble a quiet, "Fuck."

Not quiet enough.

"What's the matter?" Only, Misty doesn't give me a minute to answer before she's bouncing at my side, her hands at my arm as she peeks at my phone. "No cars because of the snow?" she sings, not even trying to sound disappointed for me. "Now you have to stay!"

And man, maybe that's just what I needed, because I'd rather walk barefoot back to the city than endure another pity-invite Christmas like the ones after my parents died.

But there's no pity in those pretty evergreen eyes peering up at me. "Look, my parents aren't supposed to be here until noon, and while they'd love for you to stay, if you want to skate out before they get here, you'll have plenty of time. But for tonight, why spend Christmas Eve alone when we could be together—" She cuts herself off and shifts uncomfortably. "Like hanging out together. Not *together* together," she finishes in a rush that makes me smile.

"You talkin' about a sleepover, Mistletoe?"

Her brows shoot high. "We've got sleeping bags. And the way we moved the furniture away from the fireplace, there's plenty of room on the rug."

I shouldn't even be thinking about it. But Misty's got her hands folded together at her chest like some hopeful little kid. "You sure?"

"Yes! Okay, let's talk Christmas movies, because we're watching one."

5

Misty

Noel agreed to stay, and now, as absurd as it seems, we're having a sleepover on the floor in front of the fire tonight. And more important than me getting more time with this man I'm not ready to give up, Noel isn't going to spend Christmas Eve alone. Neither of us will.

"How's it look now?" Noel asks, arm stuck in the tree up to his shoulder.

"Perfect." I take a picture and set my phone aside to grab a cracker off the charcuterie board we made from goodies found in my foodie mother's pantry and freezer.

Noel's already eaten three of the merlot-flavored dried salami croissant sandwiches I've made him, each one vanishing within a bite or two and eliciting this grateful masculine moan that stirs thoughts I'm not sure I should be thinking.

When I've assembled another sandwich for him, I turn back and stop.

"Um, Noel, what's going on with your hair?"

"What's wrong with it?"

His hair is pretty great. It's dark and thick and falling in loose curls around his face. Except for the two spots where it's sticking out like branches from the top of the tree. "I think you've got some sap in your hair." And by some, I mean a lot.

That lopsided smile tips in the other direction as he feels around his head, then folds altogether when he finds the clump.

"Shit."

I wave for him to follow me into the kitchen and then point to a chair. "Bring that over here and sit down. The soap probably won't do it, but I think I read something about mayonnaise, or oil. Or maybe it was nail polish remover."

"In my *hair*? During *the season*?"

Oh my God, the look on this guy's face.

"Wow. Easy there, big fella. Let me search it. But first—" I snap my fingers for the chair again, and after a beat, he pulls it over by the sink and sits while I scroll results. "Ooh, lemon essential oil!"

Peeking past my phone, I ask, "That okay for your precious tresses, or will the whole of Chicago's

Slayers fans suffer for me even suggesting such a thing?"

He shifts in the seat, heavy cheekbones tinged red. Which is so criminally cute, it gives me another one of those unfamiliar pangs in my chest. The kind I probably shouldn't be feeling for this man whose flirt knows no bounds.

"Teasing," I say, ducking into the pantry and searching the shelves until I find what I'm looking for. "Looks like the only essential oils she has are holiday blends. But I'm betting they'll still work." When I get back, Noel is tugging his shirt overhead, exposing the deep-stacked muscles of his abdomen, hard slabs of his pecs, and then those incredible shoulders.

I trip on my next step, scowling when he gives me a knowing smirk.

"Warn a girl, will you?" I pour a few drops over my fingers and set the small glass bottle beside me as the scents of orange, clove, cinnamon, and something woodsy fill the room.

"That smells really good."

"It does." Then, trying for a chill I'm not feeling, I reach for his head.

I brace for the moment my fingers touch the glossy dark strands, telling myself I'm just helping him out.

"There's... um... just two spots, really. It says to rub it in and slowly comb it through."

Another smirk. "Be gentle with me."

I ought to laugh, but the nervous energy building within me won't allow it. I rub the oil into his hair, working it in with my fingers in one section and then the other before combing a bit at a time, until a few minutes later, the teeth finally pull through.

"Think we got it."

"Yeah?"

I sift my fingers through his hair in a few places to make sure, and Noel lets out a low groan. "Feels good. You sure there isn't a little more sap in there?"

I swallow, give it another couple testing strokes, even though I'm sure. "That's it, but if you bend your head over the sink here, I'll wash it for you."

He nods and pushes out of the chair to move to the farmhouse-style sink. Resting one forearm at the side and one at the lip, he leans in close to the faucet.

"This good?" he asks from beneath a fall of dark waves.

I'm staring at the defined cut of his bare back, muscles I wouldn't have believed existed outside Photoshop, standing out in stark relief. What did he ask? Oh, right.

I nod. "That's good. Great. But, um, let me get some regular shampoo."

A shake of his head. "Dish soap is fine to get the oil out."

Right.

I turn on the water, letting it run for a few seconds to warm up, and then guide his head under to wet his hair.

"Close your eyes." I add the soap and rub it in, massaging his scalp a bit just because I know he likes it, and I like that low rumble of appreciation he makes when I do it. I use the detachable nozzle to rinse, and when he turns his head, letting the water run away from his face, his eyes open and meet mine.

The air thins until I'm not sure my knees will hold me. I turn off the water and use a clean hand towel to dry what I can of his hair before draping it around his neck.

Noel stands, using his hand to push the damp waves from his face, his fingers leaving deep ravines between the waves, then uses the towel to wipe off his shoulders and chest.

"Thanks, Misty," he says, his voice taking on a rumbling depth that wasn't there before. Was it?

I nod, looking up into his face.

Getting a little lost in the way he's looking at mine.

In how that lopsided smile slips from his lips in one of those rare serious moments.

This man is so beautiful, I forget what I was going to say. Forget about why I'm not supposed to fall for him. I forget to breathe.

And having his eyes on me like this is an addictive thing. Now that I've had it, how am I supposed to go without?

My heart stops as his eyes dip to my mouth. He shakes his head. Once. Meets my eyes again.

"Noel," I whisper a heartbeat before his mouth catches mine in a teasing, soft back-and-forth rub that incrementally deepens with every pass until—

Until it's gone in a blink, and the smile that's perpetually lifting his lips is replaced by a furrowed-brow stare so intense, I swear he can see straight into my soul.

And maybe he can.

Maybe he can see exactly how much I want this, because my name rasps low from his throat, and he pulls me in hard. Our mouths meet in a kiss that's pure combustion. Nothing tentative now. No hesitation. Just heat and need and a kind of maddening relief that somehow leaves me desperate for more.

Opening beneath the crush of his lips, I welcome his tongue, meet it with my own in a tangled, wet glide that sends heat spiraling through me, gathering in an achy knot deep in my center.

Our hands are everywhere, our bodies pressing closer and closer. My needy whimpers filling the air.

"Didn't want to push you, make you uncomfortable by hitting on you." He breathes against the side of my neck before closing his lips over the sensitive skin and sucking. "But, Christ, I've been losing my mind trying to be good."

Our mouths meet again, the kiss searing. He licks into my mouth, giving me his tongue in a slow thrust that has my hips moving restlessly against his.

His hands go to my hair, and he frees the mess of it, letting it spill down around my shoulders. One hand sifts into the strands while the other moves to my ass, kneading it with a firm touch that leaves me gasping, desperate for more.

"Mistletoe," he pants against my lips. "Tell me if you want me to slow down, to stop."

Stop?

I've never been casual about sex. I don't judge those who are. It's just not how I'm wired. But this, right now?

I shake my head. "I don't think I could stop if my next breath depended on it."

His lips curve against mine, his powerful arms pulling me tighter into his hold. "No?"

My arms link around his neck, and I shake my head.

He straightens to his full height, lifting me so my toes leave the floor. "What do you want?"

For a heartbeat, I imagine something real and lasting. I imagine years of laughter and tree farms instead of just this one. But if ever there was a guy who wasn't about *serious*, it's the man who invited me to Vegas within thirty seconds of meeting me and then spent the better part of the day referencing our engagement.

Noel isn't serious.

And I don't care because *Noel is fun*.

This day, tonight, every minute leading up to me suspended in this perfect heated bubble… has been *fun*. And I want all of it.

"I want you, Noel."

He lets out a low groan and runs that huge hand down my side, past my waist and hip, all the way to my thigh. One nudge, and I'm wrapping my legs around him tight, sifting my fingers into the damp hair at his neck, and then gasping as my back meets the fridge.

Arching, I press my shoulders into the door and my hips into the countering roll of his.

God, I can feel him between my legs. That thick, steely pressure a decadence it's been almost two years since I've had.

We shudder together, mouths fused, hearts pounding. Our eyes meet and we still. And within that single beat, the low electric charge that's been running between us, sparking with each touch and look, arcs hot and dangerous, connecting us once more.

6

Noel

Holy hell, this kiss.

It's hot and wet and greedy, and so fucking perfect I don't know that I'll ever be able to stop. Misty's whimpering around each thrust of my tongue, her fingers knotting tight in my hair like she can't get enough.

Shifting my hold, I turn us a hundred and eighty degrees to set her on the edge of the empty island. I kiss her again and grind into her heat one more time before pulling back enough to get my hand between us.

"Mistletoe, baby." I run my nose along the line of her neck to her ear. "These jeans are hot as hell on you, but they've got to go."

Evergreen eyes meet mine. Biting those kiss-swollen lips, she gives a nod and lifts her hips for me. I get her jeans off and toss them over the kitchen chair I was sitting in before. And when I turn around—

Thank you, Santa.

Rubbing a hand over the center of my chest, I swallow hard. This girl is beyond beautiful in her thin red sweater, silky green panties with a bright red bow across the front, and those creamy long legs ending in a pair of red fuzzy socks.

I kiss her again, slower this time. Just enough so we're both losing it a little when I pull away. "So, you're the gift I get to unwrap on Christmas Eve?"

She blinks up at me, eyes soft. "If you're mine."

I nod and, bracing one arm on the counter beside her, smooth the other up the curve of her sexy thigh. Hooking a couple fingers in her panties, I draw them down as she lifts again. When they're free, I tuck them into the pocket of my jeans. "For safekeeping. Or a keepsake."

I'm teasing. Sort of. But damn, when she gives me that pretty eye roll, whatever shred of control I've been hanging on to slips, and I can't wait anymore.

"Lie back for me." Catching her at the bend in her knees, I part her legs and gently push forward, bringing them up toward her torso and then spreading her wide so she's completely open to me.

I smooth my hands over her calves. "Like this. Okay?"

Her breath is coming in ragged little pants, and her cheeks match her sweater.

She nods, and I lean over her and kiss one knee and then the other.

"Noel," she whispers, making my heart thud hard in my chest.

Dropping more slow, open-mouthed kisses along the length of her inner thigh, I hum a little. "Like it when you say my name."

I more than like it. And I'm nearly there, driving myself fucking crazy by making myself wait to taste her when I've been holding back, telling myself no since the minute I met her. I suck the spot at the top of her thigh, swirling my tongue around the sensitive skin and then sucking again, harder.

She lets out a hiccupy breath, and, pretty sure I've left a mark, I give in and close that last distance. My lips brush the soft spread of her pussy, teasing and light. Then deeper.

I give her my tongue, and damn, I don't know which is sweeter, the taste of her or her soft mewls as she grabs my hair.

What I *do* know? I can't get enough of her.

Not when I add first one finger pumping in and out as I continue to nibble, kiss, and lick, and then slowly add another.

Not when she's writhing against my mouth, clenching around my fingers harder every time I use them to twist, vee, or beckon her closer to release.

Not when my name is like a mantra on her lips, and I'm coated in her need.

I still want more.

I want her as far gone as I am. I want to take her to the brink and play with her there awhile, get her so hot and close, so needy, that she begs me to let her tip over. And when she does, I want it to be the best she's ever had. I want to be the only guy who's ever gotten her there, that good.

Her back arches, tempting me with a sliver of her soft belly where her sweater has ridden up. Using my free hand, I push the thin fabric higher, bunching it above the silky swells of her covered breasts.

So hot. So perfect beneath the press of my palm and brush of my thumb. And yeah, she likes that.

I slip the green cup beneath one mound, groaning when she arches harder, giving me more of her sweet taste while begging for more of my touch.

She's so wet, her inner walls hugging and sucking at my fingers.

"Please, Noel. *Please.*"

Catching her beaded nipple, I give her the pressure and tug she's begging for.

That's all it takes.

She's over the edge, gasping and shaking as she comes hard around the fingers I gentle inside her.

Slowly, we part.

I kiss her inner thigh and then help her sit up,

my heart doing that same caveman thumping thing that's been happening since the first sharp look from those evergreen eyes. Only the look she gives me now is soft and maybe a little shy.

"That was crazy," she says breathlessly.

I nod. But it's not just crazy.

This is flat-out fucking nuts. I know it.

I don't get all tied up about most girls. Hardly any. But Misty has me in so many knots, I'm not sure I could get free if I wanted to.

She reaches for my belt, tugging me closer even though Not-So-Little-Noel is already butted up to the edge of the island.

Maybe she just doesn't want to let me go. I like that a lot.

"Come 'ere," I say, gathering her against me. Looping her arms around my neck and then wrapping her legs at my waist again and picking her up like that.

I walk her back to the living room, loving the feel of her in my hold and the damp heat of her against my bare stomach. The sleeping bags we set up are warm in front of the fire, the room lit in the flickering orange glow of the flames. I'll get something to clean up in a few minutes, but for now, I just want to lie here and hold her.

Kiss her some more like this.

Maybe get her out of that bra and spend the night watching Die Hard movies— her favorite, because this girl can't get any better —and building gingerbread houses with her in nothing but those fuzzy socks and the sweater that *barely* covers her ass.

"God, you feel so good like this," she murmurs against my lips, hands ghosting over my chest and shoulders as I half hold myself above her, half drive myself insane, giving her just enough of my weight to torture us both.

Those soft, coasting hands find their way to my belt... one going to work on it while the other finds my dick through my jeans and gives him a mind-blowing stroke.

Fuck, that's good.

It takes everything I have, but somehow, I get the words past the vise on my throat. "We gotta stop."

Misty

NOT WHAT I WAS EXPECTING. Like, at all.

"Stop?" I squeak, pulling my hands away even though Noel's still mostly on top of me and not really making any move to get off. Which is good because I don't want to lose this yet. I don't want to lose him.

I'm still sluggish and hazed from the kitchen, but I have enough brain cells working to take a stab at why this man would give me the best orgasm of my life and then be ready to beg off before getting satisfaction himself.

"Hey, if you're worried I'll get the wrong idea," I start, my voice unsteady, "I know this isn't something serious."

Noel's chin pulls back, his brows furrowing, his voice flat. "You do?"

He doesn't believe me.

That hurts a little, but I can't entirely blame him since it's not entirely the truth. I mean, yes, I *rationally* know this isn't serious. I've been having sit-down talks with myself about it all day. Still, somehow, emotionally, it's gotten a wee bit serious for me. Okay, more than a wee bit. I don't feel like this about most guys after months of dating, let alone a single day.

I didn't mean to let it happen. Heck, I didn't even think it was possible for me to fall for someone like this, but I have.

But just because I've gone and done the most stupid thing on the planet doesn't mean I think Noel would.

I meet his eyes, steeling myself against the emotion this frown he's wearing all but guarantees he won't want to see. "You invited me to fly to Vegas before you knew my name. Asked me to marry you over hot chocolate. *I get it*. You're a guy who likes to have fun but isn't looking for forever."

"You get it," he says slowly, searching my eyes. "I thought— Is that all *you're* looking for? A little fun?"

I could tell him yes. Play like I'm someone different than I am, but that's not what I want.

I want Noel to know me. I want us to be friends. So, I give him the truth— minus the whole falling-for-him-in-a-single-day thing, that is.

"Yes and no. I mean, if you were looking for something more than that, would I be interested? I would. But if you're not, I understand it." I take a shaky breath. "I've had more fun with you today than I can remember having in the last year. And even if we don't have anything more than Christmas, I want it all."

Noel's mouth tips, but that too-intense look stays in his eyes.

"Can I tell you something that not a lot of people know?"

"Yes."

"I'm actually a pretty *serious* guy. I had to be in order to get where I am in my career. I know what it means to commit and to work for what you love. And it's never bothered me, on ice or off."

I love the feel of this man on top of me, but suddenly I need to be up. I need to make sure I understand what he's saying. He sits back, runs a rough finger over my knee, then shrugs. "Yeah, I goof around... but I don't really *fool* around. I don't get physical with women I'm not interested in having something real with."

My heart skips. "But you're so *flirty*."

"*That's* just for fun. It makes people feel good, and, since it never goes anywhere, I don't lose friends over it." He takes a breath and reaches for my hand to play with my fingers. "But when I'm interested in a woman as more than a friend, I'm a *very* serious guy. So, I guess what I'm asking here is if you think you could be serious too?"

This isn't happening. He can't be for real.

Giving in to a choked laugh, I nod. Then clearing my throat, sit straighter.

"I'm actually a pretty serious girl."

"Yeah?"

God, that lopsided grin.

"And something not a lot of people know about me... This is the only time I've ever kissed a guy after the first date." Or not even a date, really.

Noel's dark brow pushes up, pulling the corner of his mouth even higher. He *tsks*. "That wasn't our first date, Mistletoe." And then, before I can blink, he ducks in and presses a firm, quick kiss to my mouth. "That was like our first five dates. More. One, we went eavesdropping together. Two, you made me hot chocolate. Then, we went out for lunch—"

"The Jimmy John's drive-thru is not—"

"Hell, yes, it is." He pulls me onto his lap and

gives me another quick kiss. "*A date*. Our *third*. A good one too."

It was good. We discovered our mutual distrust of mayonnaise. "Then we went to the tree farm."

He bites that epically kissable bottom lip. "Well, first we went out for a drive. Then our next date was at the tree farm. Then shopping together."

"Mmm. So that's six."

"See? Then there was the tree-decorating date. Seven."

God, he's fun.

"Followed by the hair-washing date. Eight."

"Always a classic."

"And then, we kissed. And…" I wave a hand through the air, indicating all the *and*. That grin says he knows exactly what I mean. "But now that we're talking about things maybe being more serious than I was giving them credit for"— I shift around until I'm straddling his lap and his big hands are cupping my ass beneath my sweater —"maybe we *shouldn't* stop."

He groans, pulling me in closer but then pressing his forehead to mine. "You don't even know how bad I want to be inside you right now. But we can't tonight."

A thought occurs to me, and I swallow hard. "Okay, are you *saving yourself* for marriage?" And then I rush on. "I mean, it's completely fine if you are. But—"

He barks out a laugh, grinning down at me. "Um, No. That ship sailed a long time ago. Misty, I stopped because I don't have a *condom*." Then, seeing my look of surprise, he laughs again. "I haven't had a girlfriend in two and a half years. Unlike a lot of the guys on my team, I don't screw around casually, so I don't carry them. But you can bet I'm going to start."

I take a breath and then squirm off his lap, immediately hating the distance between us. But this is important. I smooth my sweater down my hips. "Give me one sec."

"What are you doing?"

I start rifling through the boxes filled with presents until I find the one I'm looking for. When I come back and crawl onto Noel's lap, it's like coming home. Complete with another one of those sweet kisses.

I hold the small box wrapped in silver paper with a bright red bow between us. "Open it."

Noel cocks his head. "This has your sister's name on it."

"Ignore that. I'm re-gifting it to you. Pre-gifting? I don't know what you call it, but it's yours."

He hesitates. "What if the only thing I want is for you to maybe consider not moving with Stormy. You said you weren't that excited about Seattle, and I know it's fast, but if what you're feeling is anything even close to what I'm feeling, then—"

I press my fingers against his lips. "Seattle isn't important to me."

And God, the way he's looking at me is saying things it's too soon to put into words... but I'm feeling just the same.

That lopsided smile is back. "I don't want to rush you."

"So you're going to wait until tomorrow before you ask me to marry you again?" I tease softly.

"I'm going to try." And there's nothing teasing about the way he says it. "But even if you want the long engagement, I'm thinking I'll be able to get my ring on your finger by New Year's."

It's crazy talk, but maybe Noel's crazy isn't that far off from my own, because I'm not laughing or rolling my eyes. I'm leaning in for a slow, lingering kiss. "Okay."

He rubs his nose along mine. "Okay?"

I nod. "Yeah. But for now? I really need you to open this present."

He grins and carefully unwraps the paper and removes the bow... and lets out another laugh, louder than before. And then he pulls some move that has me wondering just how strong this guy is, because in the next breath, I'm on my back and he's on top of me, the box of Magnums I'd gotten as a joke— mostly a joke —for Stormy somehow clutched in my hands.

"That's the second-best Christmas gift I've ever gotten."

"Yeah? What's the first?"

"You, Mistletoe."

Thank you for reading DIRTY CHRISTMAS! Want more sizzling Slayers Hockey goodness? Diesel and Stormy are next up in DIRTY GROOM!

You can find out more about me, Slayers Hockey, and the rest of my books at miralynkelly.com

ALSO BY MIRA LYN KELLY

SLAYERS HOCKEY

DIRTY SECRET (Vaughn & Natalie)

DIRTY HOOKUP (Quinn & George)

DIRTY REBOUND (Rux & Cammy)

DIRTY TALKER (Wade & Harlow)

DIRTY DEAL (Axel & Nora)

DIRTY CHRISTMAS (Noel & Misty)

DIRTY GROOM (Diesel & Stormy)

BACK TO YOU

HARD CRUSH (Hank & Abby)

DIRTY PLAYER (Greg & Julia)

DIRTY BAD BOY (Jack & Laurel)

THE WEDDING DATE BOOKS

MAY THE BEST MAN WIN (Jase & Emily)

THE WEDDING DATE BARGAIN (Max & Sara)

JUST THIS ONCE (Sean & Molly)

DECOY DATE (Brody & Gwen)

COMING AROUND AGAIN (McTark Re-releases)

Just Friends (Matt & Nikki)

All In (Lanie & Jason)

ACKNOWLEDGMENTS

Fun fact: There's more to creating a book than writing the words alone. A lot more!

The magic that goes into each story that finds its way onto your eReader or shelf extends from that first willing ear past the last set of eyes checking for typos. And I am beyond grateful for every single one of the people continually proving that writing is a team sport.

So huge thanks to Lexi Ryan, Jennifer Haymore, Kara Hildebrand, Sandra Shipman, Lisa Kuhne, Crystal Perkins, Zoe York, Skye Warren, Becca Syne, Najla Qamber Designs, and my incredible agent Nicole Resciniti.

To all the girls from Write All The Words, my friends from Hockey Ever After and the PJ Party, my Promo team and Eagle Eyes, and the reviewers and bloggers who help me spread the word about my books. To my family who puts up with my crazy hours and pig pen office and my friends who are the best break from deadline crazy.

And especially to you! Thank you for reading.

((HUGS)) Mira

ABOUT THE AUTHOR

Hard core romantic, stress baker, and housekeeper non-extraordinaire, Mira Lyn Kelly is the USA TODAY bestselling author of more than two dozen sizzly love stories with over a million readers worldwide. Growing up in the Chicago area, she earned her degree in Fine Arts from Loyola University and met the love of her life while studying abroad in Rome, Italy... only to discover he'd been living right around the corner from her back home. Having spent her twenties working and playing in the Windy City, she's now settled with her husband in Minnesota, where their four amazing children and two ridiculous dogs provide an excess of action and entertainment. www.miralynkelly.com

Looking to stay in touch and keep up with my new releases, sales and giveaways?? Join my newsletter at miralynkelly.com/newsletter and my Facebook reader group at MiraLynKellyPJParty. We'd love to have you!!

Printed in Great Britain
by Amazon

47821095R00047